BUSY LITTLE BEAVER

by Dawn Bentley
Illustrated by Beth Stover

Little® Soundprints

To my parents, Dave Bentley and Sandra McKenney—
Thank you for a lifetime of love and support. I love you. — D.B.

Published by Soundprints Division of Trudy Corporation, Norwalk, Connecticut.

Book design: Marcin D. Pilchowski
Editor: Laura Gates Galvin
Editorial assistance: Chelsea Shriver

First Edition 2003
10 9 8 7 6 5 4 3 2
Printed in China

Acknowledgments:
  Our very special thanks to Dr. Don E. Wilson of the Department of Systematic Biology at the Smithsonian Institution's National Museum of Natural History for his curatorial review.
  Soundprints would also like to thank Ellen Nanney and Robyn Bissette at the Smithsonian Institution's Office of Product Development and Licensing for their help in the creation of this book.
  Many thanks to Laura Gates Galvin, my editor-extraordinaire, who made this project a joy to work on! (D.B.)

Library of Congress Cataloging-in-Publication Data

Bentley, Dawn.
  Busy little beaver / by Dawn Bentley ; illustrated by Beth Stover.
    p. cm.
  Summary: Beaver and his mate avoid dangers from a fox and an owl as they build a lodge, raise a litter of kits, and prepare for winter.
    ISBN 1-59249-011-5 (pbk.)
  1. Beavers—Juvenile fiction. [1. Beavers—Fiction.] I. Stover, Beth, 1969- ill. II. Title.

PZ10.3.B4517 Bu 2003
[E]—dc21

                                                            2002191153

Table of Contents

Chapter 1: Home, Sweet Home   5

Chapter 2: Danger at Dinner   15

Chapter 3: Beaver Babies   27

Chapter 4: More Work to Be Done   37

Glossary   44

Wilderness Facts about the Beaver   45

A note to the reader:
Throughout this story you will see words in **bold letters**.
There is more information about these words in the
glossary. The glossary is in the back of the book.

Chapter 1

Home, Sweet Home

Beaver and his **mate** walk through the woods. Beaver's mate will have babies soon.

Beaver and his mate need a home. Beaver sees a stream. They will build a **dam**.

Beaver and his mate cut down trees with their sharp front teeth. They cut branches. They pile sticks, rocks and mud across the stream.

The dam is finished in three days. Now Beaver builds a **lodge** in the still pond.

The lodge has a room for eating. It has a room for sleeping. It even has a bathroom!

Chapter 2

Danger at Dinner

Beaver is hungry. Beaver swims around the pond. He sniffs for danger. It is safe.

A porcupine passes by a tree. Beaver walks to the tree. Beaver chews the tree.

Beaver chews the tree until it falls down! He eats the tasty bark. He sniffs for danger again.

A fox is near!

Beaver runs!

Beaver sees a

hole in the

ground. Beaver

jumps in!

Beaver has built many escape holes. The holes all lead to his pond. Beaver swims to his lodge.

Chapter 3

Beaver Babies

Beaver and his mate get ready for their babies. They clean the lodge. Soon, four **kits** are born.

The kits can see
and hear. The
kits can walk
and swim.

The kits can cry, too! They are hungry. They nurse until they are full.

Beaver helps care for the kits. He watches them play. An owl flies above. The owl means danger.

Beaver warns the kits. He slaps his tail on the water. The kits swim back to the lodge.

Chapter 4

More Work to Be Done

Winter is coming.

Beaver cuts trees

into small pieces.

He piles the pieces

next to the lodge.

Soon the pond will freeze. Beaver and his family will stay in the lodge. They will eat from the food pile.

In spring, the ice will melt. Beaver and his family will swim and dive again!

In spring, more kits will be born. Beaver will make his lodge bigger. Beaver is always busy!

Glossary

Mate: one of a pair of animals that breeds to have babies.

Dam: a wall built across a stream that traps water behind it and creates a deep pond.

Lodge: a beaver home.

Kit: a baby beaver.

Wilderness Facts About the Beaver

Beavers are the largest rodents in North America. They can grow to be as big as a large dog. They can weigh between 35 and 70 pounds.

Beavers live about ten to fifteen years. They live in family units. Each beaver family has its own home with a dam, pond and lodge.

Beavers are good swimmers. They
can swim with their eyes open.
They can close their ears and noses
to keep water out. Beavers can stay
underwater for up to fifteen minutes.

Beavers have flat, scaly tails. They wag their tails from side to side to move through the water. They slap their tails on the water to warn others of danger. Beavers also use their flat tails for balance while chewing on twigs. And, beavers sit on their tails.

Animals that live near beavers in the Atlantic wilderness include:

Black bears	Porcupines
Eastern chipmunks	Raccoons
Eastern gray squirrels	Red foxes
Fishers	Striped skunks
Little brown bats	White-tailed deer
Moose	Wood frogs